To Linda, Be
& David,

CW00707039

20/12/18

The Man Who Was Different

First Published in 2018 by Catapult Books

First Edition

© Mark Currie 2018
Original story and illustrations by Mark Currie 1993
Copyright in Mark Currie's illustrations is owned by Catapult Books
All rights reserved

Published by Catapult Books

www.catapultfilms.co.uk/books

ISBN: 978-0-9568581-2-2

ACIP Catalogue of this book is available from the British Library

The Man Who Was Different

by Mark Currie

For Joe, Maisie and Jimmy.

"Be yourself. Everyone else is already taken."

Oscar Wilde

The Man Who Was Different

There was once a man who had three eyes, four legs, ears like an elephant and the loudest voice and the strongest arms of any man on earth.

His only desire was to be liked and to make other people happy.

So he set out to show himself to the world.

H

e came across a town, where
he drew a crowd of
many people.

And the people said,
"What an incredible man! Just look
at the things he can do!"

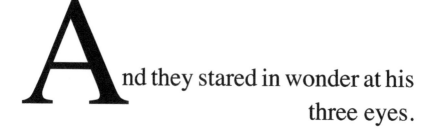

And they stared in wonder at his three eyes.

Two in the normal place and one
in the back of his head.

A

nd he showed them how he
could see things far away,
even when his back was turned.

And he claimed to see a tiger with two
heads a hundred miles away. And sure
enough when they looked, the people
saw this to be true.

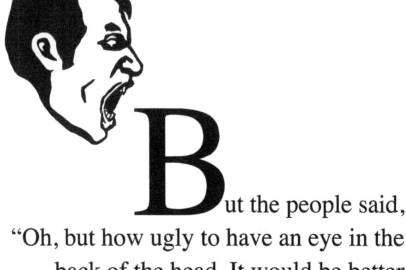

But the people said,
"Oh, but how ugly to have an eye in the
back of the head. It would be better
not to have such an eye. You
would still be an incredible fellow."

And so when enough had said it,
the man removed the eye from the back
of his head and then he had two eyes
like all other men.

And the people said, "What an incredible man! Just look at the things he can do!"

And they stared in wonder
at his four legs.
Two in the normal place and the
other two inbetween.

And he showed them how far
he could walk without
getting tired.
For if two legs grew weary, he would
rest them and use the other two.

And this way he could walk to the
edge of the world and back
in one day.

B
ut the people said, "Oh, but how silly to have four legs. It would be better not to have the inbetween legs. You would still be an incredible fellow."

And so when enough had said it,
the man removed the inbetween legs
and then he had two legs
like all other men.

A nd the people said, "What an incredible man! Just look at the things he can do!"

And they stared in wonder at his
ears like an elephant.

And he showed them how amazing his hearing could be by declaring that a leaf had fallen from a tree that was a hundred miles away. And sure enough when they looked, the people saw this to be true.

But the people said, "Oh, but how ridiculous to have ears like an elephant. It would be better not to have such ears. You would still be an incredible fellow."

And so when enough had said it,
the man removed his ears
like an elephant and then he had
ears like all other men.

And the people said, "What an incredible man! Just look at the things he can do!"

And they listened in wonder to the great loudness in his voice.

And he showed it to them by
shouting to the whole
world. And all heard him, even
those underground who were dead.
But the people said,
"Oh, but how noisy to have
such a loud voice.

It would be better not to have it
so loud. You would still be
an incredible fellow."

And so when enough had said it,
the man silenced his voice and then
he had a voice like all other men.

A nd the people said, "What an
incredible man! Just look
at the things he can do!"

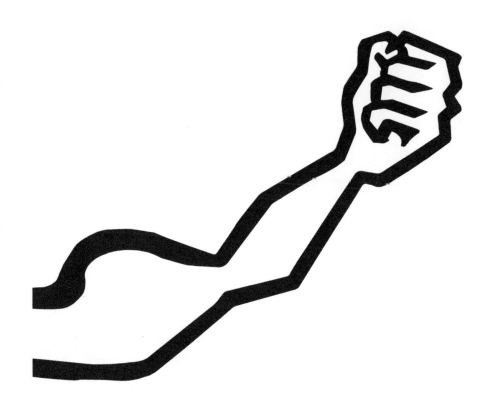

And they stared in wonder
at his mighty arms.

A

nd he showed his great strength by lifting whole buildings and towns into the air. But the people said, "Oh, but how absurd to have such mighty arms.

It would be better not to have arms so strong.
You would still be an incredible fellow."

And so when enough had said it,
the man removed his mighty arms and
then he had arms like all other men.

And then the people said,
"What is so incredible
about this man?
He is just the same as you or I."

And as the man was now just like
all other men and
had nothing left to show,
he went his way
in the world and was
never seen again.

The End

Afterword by Martin Firrell (public artist)

The Man Who Was Different is a deceptively simple fable.

Like all fables it illuminates an essential truth about human nature.

In this case, it is the truth that we are fascinated by things that are different. But also afraid of them.

We are drawn to the novelty of difference but also put into a state of alert by it. What frightens us excites us, but often in difficult and problematic ways.

The question of difference is always the question of 'different from what?' Who decides what is usual or 'normal' and therefore what deviates from that norm?

With a disheartening predictability it is usually Might that makes Right. The collective might of the majority decides who is right and who is 'wrong', who is in and who is out, who is to be targeted, bullied, oppressed, abused.

This is why so many African Americans value whiteness above their own blackness. This is why so many people straighten their hair. This is why wearing one's hair in an afro is so often a subversive political statement rather than a simple fashion statement.

The Man Who Was Different hints at the perils of being the one who is different, or set apart, from the rest of the group.

The Man encounters pressure from all sides to shed those aspects of himself that emphasise his difference. He must surrender being 'other' in order to conform. Otherwise, the fable intimates, a price will have to be paid.

There is always a price to be paid, either way. To be different is to live with immense personal risk.

Elderly women in the Middle Ages were accused of witchcraft simply because they had cats for company and talked to themselves. They were murdered by the righteous might of the majority.

Quentin Crisp was beaten in the street simply because his hair was hennaed and he was wearing lipstick.

But to conform is also to lessen oneself. To conform is to relinquish the distinguishing part of oneself, the part that is uniquely one's own. The individual becomes poorer but so does the whole of the society.

The American psychologist Rollo May said that the opposite of courage is not cowardice. It is conformity.

And this, I believe, is the central message of The Man Who Was Different.

About the author

 Mark Currie is a commercial film maker and graphic designer at Catapult Films, as well as an author. Born in 1960, he grew up in Burnley, Lancashire, studying at Burnley Art College and Manchester Polytechnic before moving to London in 1982.

He worked for various advertising agencies as an Art Director and Creative Director. In 1991, he moved with his family to Cairo in Egypt, returning to England later the same year to live and work in Bristol, before settling in Otley, West Yorkshire in 1994.

Originally written and illustrated by Mark in 1993, *'The Man Who Was Different'* is his first book of fiction.

Mark's previous books include '*Kicking Out. Heading In. (A Junior Coach's Diary of 1999-2000 football season)' published in 2000 by The Parr's Wood Press, "Once a Blue, Always a Blue" an illustrated book of Everton FC quotations & "I Am The Greatest!" an illustrated book of Muhammad Ali quotations, both published by Catapult Books in 2011.* See www.catapultfilms.co.uk/books for more details.

Lightning Source UK Ltd.
Milton Keynes UK
UKHW02n0400070918
328443UK00002B/16/P